Michael Grejniec

# Good Morning,

# Good Night

**NorthSouth**
New York / London

It is dark.

It is light.

# Good morning.

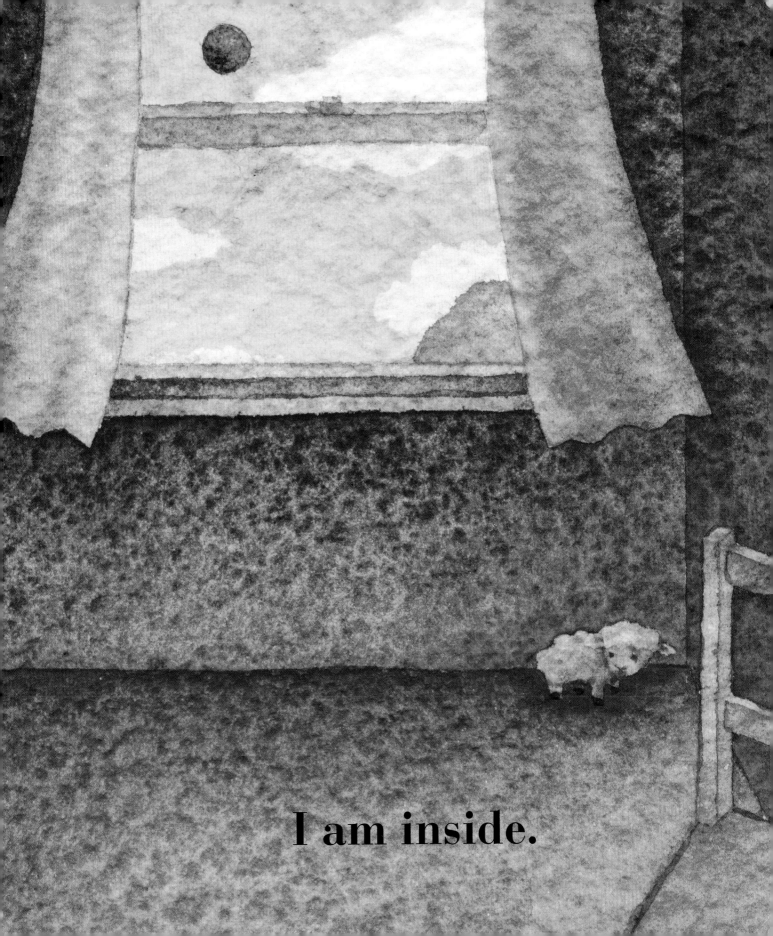

I am inside.

I am outside.

I am hiding.

I am seeking.

I have one.

I have many.

I am low.

# I am high.

It is quiet.

It is noisy.

We are far.

We are close.

Good night.

Library of Congress Cataloging-in-Publication Data
Grejniec, Michael.
Good morning, good night / Michael Grejniec.
Summary: Two children in a day of play experience such opposites
as inside and outside, hiding and seeking, and low and high.
[1. English language—Synonyms and antonyms—Fiction] I. Title.
PZ7.G8625Go 1993 [E]—de20 92-23530

A CIP catalogue record for this book is available from The British Library.

The art was painted with Pelican and Windsor Newton watercolors on Colombe paper.
The color separations were made from transparencies, rather than the original art,
so that the texture of the watercolor paper would appear in the printed book.
All the images were enlarged 250%, to accentuate the details and the
rough edges of the painting.
Book design and hand lettering by Michael Grejniec

ISBN 978-1-55858-704-5 (PAPERBACK)
5 7 9 PB 10 8 6
Printed in China

wwww.northsouth.com